Topic: Interpersonal Skills **Subtopic:** Situational Behaviors

Notes to Parents and Teachers:

As a child becomes more familiar reading books, it is important for him/her to rely on and use reading strategies more independently to help figure out words they do not know.

REMEMBER: PRAISE IS A GREAT MOTIVATOR!

Here are some praise points for beginning readers:

- I saw you get your mouth ready to say the first letter of that word.
- I like the way you used the picture to help you figure out that word.
- I noticed that you saw some sight words you knew how to read!

Book Ends for the Reader!

Here are some reminders before reading the text:

- Point to each word you read to make it match what you say.
- Use the picture for help.
- Look at and say the first letter sound of the word.
- Look for sight words that you know how to read in the story.
- Think about the story to see what word might make sense.

Words to Know Before You Read

circle
feathers
laughs
lunch
songs
spreads
story
wide

TIME TO
MOVE,
PEACOCK!
A Story About Being Still
By
J. L. Anderson
Illustrated by
Alex Willmore
Rourke
Educational Media
rourkeeducationalmedia.com

Peacock sits in a circle. The songs are nice.

He dances. He spreads his feathers out wide. Too wide.

“Stay still,” a friend says.

Peacock sits for a story. It is funny.

He laughs. He spreads his feathers out wide. Too wide.

“Stay still,” a friend says.

Peacock sits at lunch. He eats.

The food is yummy. He spreads his feathers out wide. Too wide.

"Stay still," a friend says.

Peacock sits for a show.
It is good.

He wiggles. He spreads his feathers out wide. Too wide.

"Stay still," a friend says.

Peacock sits in the gym.
Gym is fun.

He gets up. “Time to move!” his friends say.

He spreads his feathers out wide. Just wide enough!

Book Ends for the Reader

I know...

1. What does Peacock do with his feathers?
2. How do Peacock's actions affect others around him?
3. Where is Peacock when it is time to move?

I think...

1. When Peacock can't sit still during the show, do you think it's distracting for his classmates?
2. What are some times that you should be still?
3. What are some times that you can jump, wiggle, dance, and stretch your feathers?

Book Ends for the Reader

What happened in this book?

Look at each picture and talk about what happened in the story.

About the Author

J. L. Anderson lives in Texas with her family and two dogs. She loves taking her daughter to the park and reading stories together! You can learn more by visiting www.jessicaleeanderson.com.

About the Illustrator

Born in Northampton, England, in 1985, Alex has been drawing characters since the moment he first picked up a pencil.

Library of Congress PCN Data

Time To Move Peacock! (A Story About Being Still) / J.L. Anderson
(Let's Do It Together)
ISBN 978-1-64156-506-6 (hard cover)(alk. paper)
ISBN 978-1-64156-632-2 (soft cover)
ISBN 978-1-64156-742-8 (e-Book)
Library of Congress Control Number: 2018930722

Rourke Educational Media
Printed in the United States of America,
North Mankato, Minnesota

www.rourkeeducationalmedia.com

Edited by: Keli Sipperley
Layout by: Corey Mills
Cover and interior illustrations by: Alex Willmore